ANDREW HORACE BURKE

A Man for All Seasons

The Incredible Story of an Orphan Train Rider and Civil War Drummer Boy Who Grew Up to Become the Governor of North Dakota

* ✳ *

Tom Riley

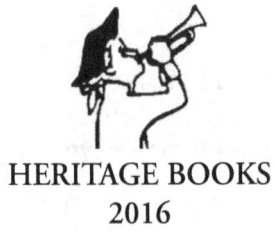

HERITAGE BOOKS
2016

HERITAGE BOOKS

AN IMPRINT OF HERITAGE BOOKS, INC.

Books, CDs, and more—Worldwide

For our listing of thousands of titles see our website
at
www.HeritageBooks.com

Published 2016 by
HERITAGE BOOKS, INC.
Publishing Division
5810 Ruatan Street
Berwyn Heights, Md. 20740

International Standard Book Numbers
Paperbound: 978-0-7884-5693-0
Clothbound: 978-0-7884-6340-2

Heritage Books by the author:

Andrew Horace Burke
A Man for All Seasons: The Incredible Story of an
Orphan Train Rider and Civil War Drummer
Boy Who Grew Up to Become the
Governor of North Dakota

Happy Valley School: A History and Remembrance

Orphan Train Riders: A Brief History of the Orphan
Train Era (1854–1929) with Entrance Records
from the American Female Guardian
Society's Home for the Friendless
in New York
Volume One

Orphan Train Riders: Entrance Records from the
American Female Guardian Society's Home
for the Friendless in New York
Volume Two

The Orphan Train to Destiny

TABLE OF CONTENTS

FOREWORD

*A*ndrew Horace Burke: A Man for All Seasons is a historical novel about the life of Andrew Horace Burke, who was orphaned at the age of four in New York City when his mother died during childbirth and his father was killed in an industrial fire. He was sent to the Children's Aid Society and, at the age of nine, rode an Orphan Train to Indiana along with John Green Brady, who later became governor of the Alaska Territory.

Burke joined the Civil War at the age of twelve as a drummer boy for the 75th Indiana Regiment. Because we know little about the battles he fought in, I have imagined his life as a drummer boy and medic during the war. From his discharge to his return to Indiana, everything is historically accurate.

This book is a companion volume to *The Orphan Train to Destiny: The Life of John Green Brady*. The fact that two boys who became fast friends should rise to governorship: Burke to become the governor of North Dakota and Green to become the governor of Alaska is an incredible coincidence. It is a tribute to the character of Burke and Brady, and, a tribute to the greatness of America.

If you enjoy this book and want to know more about the Orphan Train Era (1853–1929), please go to my website: theorphantrainriders.com. There you will have the opportunity to purchase other books on the era. I'm available for speaking engagements and to show a lecture/video on the Orphan Train Era and The Great

Hunger in Ireland (1845–1852). You can email be at totrwriter@aol.com or through my website.

CHAPTER I

Andrew Horace Burke

Andrew Horace Burke was born in New York City on May 15th, 1850. His mother died during childbirth. Both his mother and father had just arrived in New York City aboard a Coffin ship fleeing the Great Hunger in Ireland. Already weakened from a starvation diet and the eighty-five day voyage to the Staten Island Marine Hospital, her heart (misshapen from the lack of nutrition) gave way. She weighed only ninety-three pounds at her death. She was buried in a hastily dug grave in the back of an already bursting-at-the-seams cemetery. In less than a month, the occupants of the cemetery grave sites were dug up and cast into the Atlantic to keep up with the endless stream of dead and dying victims arriving in the Promised Land.

Within several days, Horace Burke and his newborn child had found refuge in a Settlement House run by The American Female Guardian Society, a Temperance agency dedicated to rescuing the impoverished and homeless children wandering the streets of New York. At any one time, over 20,000 homeless street Arabs were inhabiting alleyways, sewer pipes and boxes in a city where no social safety net existed and the law of the jungle was alive and well. The AFGS immediately helped Horace get a job as a custodian in a clothing factory and provided sustenance and shelter to his infant son. Horace would give a small stipend to the AFGS monthly out of his meager earnings and the AFGS gave him housing and food on Sundays and fed his son and sheltered him while Horace worked.

New York City in the 19th century could be a brutal place for a child. A magnet to immigrants and the poor in search of jobs, the city was also a haven for gamblers, thieves and murderers. When adults fell victim to alcoholism, prostitution or drug addiction, their children were the ones who suffered the most. Temperance organizations such as the American Female Guardian Society stepped in, establishing orphanages and homes for unwed mothers and battered women.

In 1854, when Andy was four years old, Horace Burke was killed in a factory fire. The Exit doors to his workplace had been sealed to prevent workers from leaving after 5 pm. He died along with thirty-eight other workers and was buried in Potter's field. When the AFGS learned of his death they placed Andrew Horace Burke in the newly opened Children's Aid Society on 23rd Street. When he was five he moved to the The Children's Aid Society Newsboys House where he was assigned a paper route and contributed daily to his room and board. While he was there John Brady who was three years older took him under his wing and showed him the ropes and protected him from harsh treatment by the older boys.

Burke's life was a brutal struggle for survival. Like other ragamuffins or street merchants, homeless children worked in mills, collected rags, sold newspapers or begged. They hawked matches or gum on street corners, shined shoes, ate out of trashcans, or stole food or items to sell to junk shops. Having a newspaper route saved him from utter poverty, and winding up in prison, as children as young as seven were treated as adults. Twelve-year olds and older could be put to death for theft. Those not working as newsboys slept in doorways or cardboard boxes on steam grates, in empty buildings or wherever they could find an undisturbed spot.

To make money to pay for his room and board at the Children's Aid Society lodging house, Burke sold *The Tribune* at an assigned corner in New York City. Dorothy A. Lund Nelson writes in *Burke's Journey* that each day "the oldest paperboys would sound out the words of the headlines for the five-year olds, who couldn't read. When Burke had the correct words, he would go to his corner and yell, 'Extra, extra, read all about it,' finishing his shout with the headline for the day, "taught to him by the older boys."

"Each lodging house provided clean beds," writes Alice K. Flanagan in *The Orphan Trains*, "a dining room and a reading room filled with newspapers, books and Bibles." Eventually Burke learned to read the short sentences found under the photographs or in boxes in the paper. Burke worked as a newsboy until he was nine years old. By this time, Charles Loring Brace's Children's Aid Society had begun "placing out" orphan. "Brace's idealized view believed the West had plenty of food with good-hearted and generous people," writes Rene Wendinger. He was certain Westerners would accept homeless children to help with daily chores.

In 1859, Burke was placed on an orphan train along with seventy-eight other boys and girls. He was nine years old and accompanying him was his friend, John Brady. The train headed west, stopping in town after town, essentially peddling the children. "The two boys had a lot in common," writes Stephen O'Connor in *Orphan Trains*, "not only their Irish catholic background, their institutionalization, and their shared anxieties and hopes about what would happen to them in their new homes, but also their unusual intelligence and determination. Their friendship strengthened and they became fast friends on their ride, and would stay in touch with each other throughout their lives. Perhaps by mutual influence, they would end up fulfilling startlingly

3

similar destinies"—Burke as governor of North Dakota and Brady as governor of the Territory of Alaska.

At each stop, the youngster were examined, and some chosen, "A good looking boy with a sunny disposition," writes Annette Fry in *The Orphan Trains*, "Andy Burke received several offers of a home when he reached Noblesville," Indiana.   Eventually Burke went to a farming couple from the area.

Later, Burke wrote about the long railway ride, "on the Erie route, the tearful eyes, the saddened hearts, the arrival at Noblesville on that clear, sun shining day, the dread I experienced on awaiting to be selected by one of those who had assembled in the Christian church at that place, and how my heart was gladdened by Mr. D. W. Butler, for his appearance indicated gentleness.   All those scenes will live in memory."

Life on the farm was hard and there were many chores to be done.   On Burke's tenth birthday he was given a small horse and a plow and became part of the family.   Mr. Butler and his wife had no children and during that first year he was doted upon and warmly accepted.   With the extra help Mr. Butler expanded his farm and a good part of the day Andy was plowing the new fields and harvesting their bounty.   The second year at the farm there was a drought and the pressure to make up for the shortage forced Mr. Butler to remove Andy from school and increase the acreage he had to plow.

When Andy turned twelve, all the talk at the dinner table turned toward the Civil War.   Mr. Butler felt that the newly elected President was antagonizing the South needlessly by calling for the end of slavery.   Mr. Butler had been born in Kentucky so his sympathies were for the newly elected Jefferson Davis and the Confederacy. Burke had read avidly about Lincoln and admired his

4

compassion and stand against slavery. He kept silent during Mr. Butler's tirades against Lincoln and his call for more troops to be aligned against the Confederacy. Butler sensed young Burke's empathy toward the Union and a growing divide manifested itself in silence at the table and Butler's criticism of Burke's work habits and lack of appreciation for all the Butler family had done for him. In the morning, when he had breakfast, Mrs. Butler would recount for him each item of food he was eating and their cost to the household. Andy longed to be on his own and away from the increasing alienating feelings toward the Butler's.

In Noblesville, Major John Thomas was recruiting soldiers for the 75th Indiana Regiment. Although only twelve years old Andy Burke had hardened his body due to the rigors of farm work and was planning to enlist in the regiment. Things had gotten worse at home and he felt he would soon be expelled from the household. He stopped abruptly after four hours of plowing and left the horses in the field and went off to join the Civil War on the Union side. He pleaded with Major Thomas in Noblesville to accept him as a drummer boy for the regiment. After much cajoling Thomas pointed out the dangers he would experience and relented and signed him on. As luck would have it the regiment was due to leave that very day for a thirty-day march to South Carolina. The regiment would train for three hours every day until they arrived at the battlefield in Charleston, South Carolina. Burke was excited with all the patriotic fervor and the huge crowd that had gathered to see the regiment off.

Meanwhile back at the farm, Mr. Butler found the horses in the field and cursed the day he had taken in Andy Burke.

CHAPTER II

Andy Goes To War

"**I**t's no picnic, boy, war is hell! Why do you think I'm mustering out? Soon as we get to New Bern, I'm outta here! You better learn these drum rolls fast, because in another 80 miles we'll be at my farm. All this hooting and hollering and this fake patriotic send-off don't mean nothing when you come face to face with these secessionist boys who are dead set on blowing you apart. I've had my fill of war and never want to set my eyes on another dead man. I seen too much in the battlefield, young men bloated twice their size before being rolled into a trench and covered in lime. Why the hell you left your farm for this is beyond me.

Young Andy Burke listened in rapt attention as Drum Major Billy Johnson recounted his memory of the numerous battles he'd been in and led the charge and managed to escape with just minor wounds. "It's a miracle I'm still alive, I gotta admit when it got too rough I wasn't obligated to stay in the fight since I had no weapon, I'd lead and as soon as the shooting started, go back to the ranks and lead another batch of men to their slaughter. I'm going back to my wife and kids and God's good earth, never to see another good man blown apart by cannon fire or decapitated by a sword.

"I've participated in too many mass funerals, the biggest being after Shiloh where we buried 5,000 men, many bloated twice their size. On the morning of April 6th, 1862 over 40,000 Confederate soldiers under the command of General Sydney Johnston poured out of the nearby woods and struck a line of Union soldiers occupying ground near Pittsburg Landing on the Tennessee River. The overpowering Confederate offensive drove the unprepared Federal forces from their camps and threatened to overwhelm Ulysses S. Grant's entire command. Some Federals made determined stands and by afternoon, they had established a battle line at the sunken road known as The Hornet's Nest. Repeated Rebel attacks failed to conquer but massed artillery helped turn the tide as Confederates surrounded the Union troops and captured and killed, or wounded most. By the next morning Grant's counteroffensive overpowered the weakened Confederate forces. The two day battle at Shiloh produced more than 23,000 casualties and was the bloodiest battle in American history at its time. That's another one of your duties Drummer Boy, you have to help with the stretcher bearing, look around the battlefield and bring the wounded to medical care. Then you gather the dead, help with digging the trenches and sending them off to their God. I'm mustering out and it's not too soon enough for me. I got this rash down my arm and the Doc's afraid it's going to spread to the rest of the troops so he giving me a medical discharge."

Billy taught Andy the different drum rolls and marches he would need to lift the men's spirits and drown out the musket balls whizzing by them. The drums kept the troops together in the noise and confusion of battle. It was often impossible to hear the officer's orders, so each order was given a series of drumbeats to represent it. Both soldiers and drummers had to learn which drumroll meant "meet here" and which meant "attack now" and which meant "retreat" and all the other commands of battlefield and camp. The most exciting drum call was "the long roll," which was the signal to attack. The drummer would just beat-beat-beat and every other drummer in hearing distance would beat-beat-beat until all that could be heard was an overwhelming thunder pushing the army forward.

The Civil War is sometimes called "The Boys' War" because so many soldiers who fought in it were still in their teens. The rule in the Union Army was that soldiers had to be eighteen to join, but many younger boys answered "I'm over eighteen, sir," when the recruiter asked. Many young boys marched off to war looking for adventure but they found hard, dangerous work along with it. One boy, Johnny Clem was as young as nine when he was finally accepted by Michigan troops and adopted as their mascot and drummer boy. By the time he was eleven he enlisted as a regular soldier and spent much of his life in the Army. He was a Brigadier general when he retired in 1915.

The drummer boy was the "radio-telephone operator" of his day. It was the most effective way for commanders to relay their orders to hundreds or even thousands of troops on the battlefield. "It takes your mind off the arduous task of long distance marching, if you hear something. It calms the savage beast and gives you a little heart. You are out there on the firing line and you hear something that makes you think of home or makes you think of your comrades."

Life as a drummer boy was hard. William Bircher, who enlisted in the 2nd Minnesota Regiment in the summer of 1861 after several rejections kept a diary describing the hardships of war. "We went without hot meals for weeks at a time, marching for miles without shoes and there was dysentery-and-of course-the fear and horror of battle" he shared with the regular soldiers. William didn't just play the drums, he marched, he regularly pulled guard duty and he helped with the wounded. "Our band was detailed to assist the nurses in taking care of the wounded (after the battle of

Chattanooga)," he wrote, September 22, 1863. "It was heartwarming to see the poor fellows as they were brought in, shot and mangled in every possible way. Every few minutes we had to take one out who died, and put him in the dead house, where he would remain until there was a wagonload."

During Sherman's March through Georgia, William's regiment lost another drummer: "We lost poor Simmers, the drummer of Company G, during the night. The poor fellow, being unable to keep up, lay down somewhere along the road, and was captured by the Confederates that were following us up. I took his blanket and drum to relieve him, but he was too fatigued to follow, saying "Oh, let me rest. Let me sleep a short time. Then I will follow on." I tried to keep him under my eyes, but he finally eluded me, and when we again stopped for a short rest, he was not to be found. By that time he was most likely a prisoner."

The drums were heavy and often it was too much for a small boy. There would be so much patriotic fervor and it was an avenue out of poverty for orphans and poor boys. They could earn $13 a month. There are even accounts of drummer boys who had to assist surgeons during amputations and were often asked to carry away the severed limb for disposal.

It is estimated that there were over 40,000 field musicians in the drum corps. Most were under the legal age of eighteen. Many of these boys dropped their drums and picked up weapons. The Civil war was often nicknamed, "the drummer boys' war." Most drummer boys had to learn eighteen different signals, calling units to formations, regulating meals and other daily events.

CHAPTER III

Two Years Later

Andy Burke was in the thick of it. Ulysses S. Grant had been appointed Commander of the Union Army and things began to change. Battles such as Shiloh, where troops had distained digging trenches and rifle pits and instead stood in ranks, seemed part of another war. Grant appointed Sherman and many other strong leaders. For the last six months, the drummer boy was pulling alternate duty as a surgeon's assistant as the 75th Regiment joined William Tecumseh Sherman as he advanced northward from Savannah, Georgia, through the Carolinas, with the intention of linking up with Union forces in Virginia. On February 17, Columbia surrendered to Sherman and the young Burke had been wounded by a bullet in the lower intestines. He made his way back to camp and asked the surgeon to remove the shrapnel as it was becoming infected. The surgeon flatly refused, as stomach wounds were often considered fatal and the Doctor feared Burke might die in the operation.

Burke felt he surely was going to die unless the bullet was removed. With the assistance of a young widow nurse he had made up his mind to operate on himself. "I told her my plans, that I was dying inch by inch every day. She agreed to help me. I told her to get some carbolic acid, two pairs of scissors, hot water, a sharp knife and a blunt curved hook, needles and cat-gut sutures. I placed a bullet between my teeth to bite while doing the work, for I knew it would hurt badly.

"I took the blunt curved hook and slowly introduced it in the wound, slowly twisting it as I probed deeper. I felt I had gotten the hook over the bowel and drew the bowel toward the opening. Cold perspiration was pouring off my face. I pulled more of the bowel out of the hole until I saw the bloody opening in my intestine. With my sterile fingers I felt for the slug as it had moved three inches forward in the intestines. I worked it up toward the bloody opening and removed it. I placed a roll of bandages around the intestine to keep it from slipping back into the bowel cavity. The widow handed me the curved, threaded needle and I placed six stitches in my bowel. I had to do this finely so there would be no bleeding in my gut. I closed the skin over it and stitched 8 more stitches. I took a sponge, moistened it and bathed the area of clotted blood. I looked at the face of this beautiful heroic woman, then everything went black. When I awoke 10 hours later, the Surgeon harassed me for being so foolish as to operate on myself. The nurse brought me supper and my recovery was uninterrupted. Most Surgeons regarded bowel wounds as necessarily fatal. When I was wounded I had not drawn upon my rations, I feel certain that had I been well fed my wound would have killed me."

Two months later Andy resumes his duties as drummer boy having been banned as a surgeon's assistant for life. Union forces were overwhelmed by throngs of liberated Federal prisoners and emancipated slaves. Many soldiers took advantage of ample supplies of liquor in the city and began to drink. Fires began in the city, and high winds spread the flames across a wide area. Most of the central city was destroyed, and the city's fire companies found it difficult to operate in conjunction with the invading Union army, many of whom were trying to put out the fire. Many claimed the fires were set by retreating Confederate soldiers who lit bales of cotton on their way out of town. On that same day, the Confederates evacuated Charleston. On

February 18th, Sherman's forces destroyed virtually anything of military value in Columbia, including railroad depots, warehouses, arsenals and machine shops.

"We continued to march South into Georgia to our goal Atlanta, the center of the South's industrial heart and the powerhouse of production. General Sherman's plan was to utterly destroy the industrial heart and hasten the end of the war. At some point I fell behind our unit and just wanted to sleep. We had been marching for two days. When I could go no further I sighted a large Georgia pine and threw myself on the soft matted pine needles where I fell fast asleep. Several hours later I was awakened by a band of Confederates and marched off to Andersonville Prison," said Andy.

Andersonville held more prisoners at any given time than any other Confederate military prison. During the fourteen months it existed, more than 45,000 Union soldiers were confined there. Of these, 13,000 died from disease, poor sanitation, malnutrition, overcrowding or exposure to the elements. The prison pen was surrounded by a stockade of hewed pine logs that varied in size from fifteen to seventeen feet and enclosed 261 acres. Sentry boxes stood at ninety-foot intervals. A branch of Sweetwater Creek, called the Stockade Branch, flowed through the prison yard and it was the only source of water for most of the prison. In an emergency, eight small earthen forts outside the prison could hold artillery to put down disturbances within the prison and to defend against any Union cavalry attack.

The first prisoners were brought there in late February 1864. By the end of June 26,000 men were penned in an area meant to house 10,000. By August the population swelled to 33,000. The Confederate government could not provide adequate housing, food, clothing or medical care to their Federal captives because of deteriorating economic conditions in the South and a poor transportation system.

"There is so much filth about the camp that it is terrible trying to live here," said one prisoner. "With sunken eyes, blackened faces from pitch pine smoke, rags and disease, the men look sickening. The air reeks with nastiness, I never saw such misery."

The Civil War's greatest killer was disease. Two hundred thousand Yankees and Rebels died or were mortally wounded, but nearly 400,000 died of such things as dysentery, typhoid, pneumonia (the pneumonia death rate among Confederates was 400 per 1,000 men). With 30,000 prisoners jammed into Andersonville, the death rate was 100 a day. In one year 13,000 men died.

One day Andy was asked to assist in carrying a stretcher bearing the body of a man who had died in camp. He dug a grave and presided over short prayers when a sudden disturbance broke out within the camp. It was a fight over meager scraps of food. Even the guard accompanying them left to quell the disturbance. Andy saw his chance and raced for a stand of pines. He ran for three miles through the forest. A drizzle began and he sought refuge under a pine. He was cold, hungry and exhausted and his heart was pounding. He longed for food as he now weighed less than eighty-eight pounds. He crawled to a gully to keep a low profile as now and then a passing contingent of Confederates passed by singing Rebel songs. He decided he would only travel by nightfall to avoid the Rebels. After about a week he had reached a huge contingent of Union soldiers stationed on Hilton Head in South Carolina. He described conditions at Andersonville, was fed all he could eat and slept for two days.

When he awoke he immediately went to the Colonel and pleaded with him to be discharged. "I've served two and a half years and I've had my fill of war. I took a bullet in Georgia, spent three months in Andersonville, almost starved to death. I'm only fourteen having enlisted as a Drummer Boy with the 75th Regiment in Indiana. I want to make my way back to Indiana. I've served my country to the best of my ability. I'm sick and tired of the glory of war and my soul needs rest and peace," said Andrew.

"Boy you have submitted your request to the rightful authority. You are a soldier and must remain a soldier until you are properly discharged. If you attempt to leave without orders, it will be mutiny and I will shoot you like a dog. Go back into the fort now and don't leave without my consent. Having been separated from the 75th Indiana, you are now a soldier of our Regiment and we're going to Hilton Head to join the Union Army garrisoned there, 30,000 strong," said Colonel Burnside.

CHAPTER IV

The Battle for Hilton Head

"The choice being made to attack the Confederacy in the Deep South via a Union fleet started when we boarded sixty ships and arrived off the coast of Beaufort, South Carolina. The naval force was under the command of Admiral DuPont and we operated under the direction of General T. W. Sherman (no relation to Tecumseh). We attacked Fort Walker on Hilton Head and Beauregard at Bay Point. By 3 pm we fired 3,000 shots at the two forts and the Confederate forces retreated, leaving the Beaufort area to Union forces."

This battle set the Sea Island Blacks free and was the beginning of their long road to freedom. The fall of Hilton Head was the single greatest event in their lives and Sam Mitchel, at the age of eighty-seven, remembered the event vividly. "Maussa had nine children, six boys in the Rebel army. When I heard the shooting I thought it was thunder but that day there was no clouds. My mother say, 'son that ain't no thunder, that's Yankees come to give you freedom.' I jump up and down for joy. The Maussa ordered my father to get his row boat and carry him to Charleston. My mother told my father, 'you ain't gonna row no boat to Charleston. You go out that back door and keep going.'" Within two days of the Union victory, the Sea Island Blacks began descending on the Union outpost. One Union soldier said, "negro slaves came flocking into the camp by the hundreds, escaping from their masters when they knew of the landing of Lincoln soldiers. Many of them had no clothing but gunny-sacks."

General Sherman wrote the War Department asking for humanitarian assistance. And missionaries, known as Gideon's Band came to Hilton Head and began teaching and helping the Blacks. The Secretary of the Treasury, Salmon P. Chase was a strong anti-slavery voice in Lincoln's Cabinet and he sent a lawyer, Edward Pierce, to Hilton Head. Land was given to the slaves and they established their own villages. Schools were established, a mayor and treasurer and marshal were elected and the town became known as Mitchelville. The population was 1,500. Stores opened and merchandise was for sale. Methodist, Baptist and Presbyterian churches were established. Many of the free men in Mitchelville worked for the Union army.

Andy being young befriended a slave, named Joseph and was invited to his home during a funeral for a highly respected relative. "I learned death to an African American is not an event to be 'handled' and then forgotten about. When one dies, there is a series of events which usually take place. Family members are notified right away. An old belief is that the dead can't be buried on a rainy day. The Devil will take his soul. The family often attempts to bury the dead on a sunny day. There is usually a five to seven day mourning period before the funeral takes place and it is often at the home of the deceased. There is lots of food cooked by family members and memories are shared about the deceased. It is important the dead be buried facing East to allow rising at Judgment Day. Coins are placed on the eyes of the dead to keep them closed. Coins are also placed in and around the grave as a token of admittance into the Spirit World."

When General William T. Sherman and his army of 62,000 men approached the South Carolina border, he ordered a "scorched earth policy." This total war strategy, though brutal was believed to cause mass desertion among Confederate troops and break the South's will to fight. "We were taken aboard ships to the mouth of the Tulifinny River along with 900 Marines. We landed near the town of Yemassie. The objective was to destroy a railroad trestle that crossed the Tulfinny River. I met with the Drummer Boys of the New York Infantry, the Ohio Infantry, the Rhode Island Infantry and the 32nd U.S. Colored Troops and the 33rd U.S. Colored Troops. We wanted to coordinate as much as we could our drum rolls.

"We were told that for the first time we'd be facing cadets from the Citadel Academy who were deployed to defend the state. Under cover of darkness the entire force of cadets gathered their muskets and ammunition, fixed their bayonets and prepared to attack. A surprise attack ensued and it drove the Union forces back several hundred yards to their trenches. Further attacks made us retreat and we followed the Tulfinny River southward. It would take Sherman and his troops to burn and take the Citadel Academy.

"I finally reunited with 75th Regiment on Dufuskie Island near Hilton Head Island. My Regiment had lost 232 men, many of whom had died from disease. It was great to see my comrades again, however I was sick and tired of war and was actually experiencing loss of weight, lack of energy and a persistent swelling of my lymph glands under my arms and near my neck. I was also experiencing night sweats and nightmares. I went to see Commander Thomas and asked to be given an Honorable Discharge and a stipend for my disability. I had served three years and seven months and longed to be discharged.

"I was led to his tent and was so nervous I forgot my prepared speech. General Thomas grabbed my shoulders and said, 'How are you Andy? I thought we lost you when the Confederates captured you. How did you manage to escape?'

"I spent three months in Andersonville and went down to eighty-eight pounds. I was on a burial details and a disturbance broke out in the camp. The guard went back to quell it and I took off. I lived in the swamps for five days. Before that I took a bullet in the stomach. I've served three years seven months and have been involved in twelve battles and numerous skirmishes. My physical health is weakening steadily and my lymph glands are always swollen. I have nightmares and the sweats and don't think I can do my duties anymore. The drum even feels heavier each day. General, I'm asking to be given an Honorable Discharge and even a small stipend for my suffering. I would be most grateful if you would grant my request," said Andy.

"Andy when you joined I told you no, but you insisted and I gave in. You were only twelve years old and now we are here three and a half years later and I see before me a man in everything but age. You have performed admirably and I'm so glad you survived Andersonville. I will grant your request, award you the appropriate medals. I will also requests from the Commander-in-Chief a pension for the time you have served our Blessed Union. Tomorrow at noon I will have your Honorable Discharge ready and you can go back to civilian life knowing you have served your country admirably."

CHAPTER V

Dufuskie Island

General Thomas, concerned about my physical deterioration decided to give me two weeks rest and relaxation before I boarded a mail packet ship back to Baltimore. I boarded a small boat to see my Gullah friend, Joseph to let him know I was returning to Indiana. We had gotten close since I attended the funeral so I was invited to share a dinner of the most delicious gumbo I ever tasted. The Army food I was constantly eating had only added twenty pounds on my frame, so I wanted to get back to my fighting weight of 125 pounds before I returned to Noblesville.

As we ate, Joseph told me about his family. "My people came from Angola in West Africa. We were brought here as slaves by the British 100 years ago. In Angola we had been rice farmers for centuries and many of our dishes are rice based. They brought us to the Low Country to farm rice because many of the white people were getting yellow fever and malaria. We had grown an immunity to these diseases because we have been farming rice for thousands of years. We were the first slaves freed when the Union Army garrisoned 30,000 troops on Hilton Head Island. Many Gullah people have served with distinction in the Union Army; my brother, Abraham is in Pennsylvania. Missionaries from Pennsylvania came down here and started schools for us several years ago. That's why my English is good. Our school is called Penn Center," said Joseph. I spent the most pleasant evening with that close family and I shared with them my own story. They invited me to stay with them as long as I liked. I told Joseph I would make an effort to see him again one day. That I had to go back to Noblesville, attend college and make my way in the world.

I had applied to be accepted at Asbury College in Noblesville since I was eligible for G.I. Benefits from President Lincoln. My friend and fellow orphan train rider, John Brady, who was four years older than me and in his third year at Yale University, believed I could really benefit from a college education. "It prepares you for change and you're able to adjust to any circumstances. With all you've been through at such a young age I predict great things are ahead for you. You've seen the worst of mankind; with education you can make all things better." I looked forward to the encouraging letters from my friend. In fact they were the only letters I ever received.

I had time to think about what I wanted to do with the rest of my life. I would walk the beach at Hilton Head sometimes accompanied by a dolphin offshore who kept pace with me. I realized I was good with numbers; maybe banking was in my future. I knew in some small way I wanted to change the world for the better. My friend, John says he wants to get into politics. He was taken in by Judge Green and probably learned a lot. He says he's also interested in being a missionary and a lawyer. I guess education does prepare you to have a lot of choices.

I spent time building up my body and running along the beach. There was a tough world out there and I wanted to be ready for it. I still had nightmares and night sweats and prayed for all the young soldiers I had seen cut down in their teenage years. I was determined to become somebody because I was given life and know how precious it is. I also longed to meet a nice girl and get married someday.

CHAPTER VI

Back at Noblesville he attended Asbury College and took business courses and accounting. He still had trouble sleeping and severe headaches. He had almost constant nightmares and they were always on the same theme. There would be a battle and all of a sudden, the land would give way and he was constantly running back to safety to prevent being swallowed up by the landslide. After strong coffee in the morning the headaches would give way and he attended classes. He was now sixteen years old and many of his classmates did not know about his war time experiences. After classes he went to a saw mill and cut wood for eight hours to earn money.

In his second year in college, he began to experience extreme tiredness and went to a local doctor. The nightmares didn't let up and the headaches increased in intensity. At first the local doctor felt he had tuberculosis and recommended he go to a sanitarium but Burke refused. He knew it was unresolved issues from the war, feelings of guilt, survivor's guilt and post-traumatic stress. He decided to drop out of college for a while and he accepted an offer to write for The *Evansville Courier* newspaper. After six months on the job he was asked to cover the final months of the Civil War but he turned down the assignment, not wanting to experience further nightmares. He was let go. Eventually he moved to Minneapolis and found work as a laborer. While there he met Caroline "Carrie" Cleveland, and they were married in 1879. A year later, Burke and his bride moved to Castleton, Dakota Territory, sporting $65 in his pocket. He found work as a bookkeeper with Hibbard and Parlin, who operated a General Store. It was there that he made important connections to Republican Party leaders.

Burke was elected Cass County treasurer twice, and when the state's first governor, John Miller decided not to seek re-election, Burke became the unanimous nominee of the Republicans. He was popular when he first became governor. The rags to riches story about a street orphan from New York who rose to become a state governor was printed in newspapers across the United States.

The new governor was even offered Alexander McKenzie's huge Bismarck house to use as a residence. During Burke's tenure, laws were enacted to authorize $150,000 in state bonds to pay North Dakota's share of the indebtedness of the Territory of Dakota. Also enacted were a general election law, one to promote irrigation, and a law empowering the governor to appoint a commission to compile the laws.

"This commission," writes C. A. Lounsberry in *History of North Dakota*, "discovered...there was no law for the election of presidential electors. The absence of which debarred the people from voting for the President.... And others. A hastily called special session of the Legislature solved the problem."

<hr>

During his first year, the state was visited by the Rocky Mountain Locust, Melanophus spretus, as well as nineteen other species of the huge grasshoppers, some up to four inches. According to the U.S. Department of Agriculture, this species had entered North Dakota the previous fall from the northwest...just east of the Turtle Mountains, and leaving the first batch of eggs near Cando.

Luckily, the locust could be fought. Not only did Burke recommend state money to be spent to exterminate the insects; but used some personal money. Using mixtures of arsenic with wheat bran or molasses and sawdust, 20,000 acres of wheat alone were saved, worth some $400,000.

CHAPTER VII

Tension and Strife

Railroad baron, Alexander McKenzie asked Burke to veto a bill which had been passed by the 1891 Legislature and favored by the Farmers Alliance, "that required railroads to lease sites on the right of way, for the construction of elevators and warehouses to store grain. These facilities were to be free from unfair practices on the parts of the railroads." Burke considered the bill unconstitutional. Many Alliance members quit the Republican Party and started their own, putting up their own candidate, Eli Shortridge, for governor. Burke had angered enough people that he lost the governorship to Shortridge.

Burke attempted a foray into the grain dealership in Duluth, Minnesota, but so many farmers were angry with him that he did not do well, unlike former Governor John Miller, who had made a fortune at it. Burke was appointed Inspector for the U.S. Land Office in Washington, D.C., in 1895.

Burke was assigned to the Land Office in Roswell, New Mexico. He had two twin daughters, Mrs. Amy Burke Johnson of Clayton, New Mexico and Mrs. Ada Burke Mrkvicka of Superior, Arizona.

Andrew Burke died on Wednesday, November 27th, 1918. He was sixty-eight. They attended to him in his last hours. His wife had passed away a year earlier.

This eulogy appeared in *The Weekly Star* of Roswell, New Mexico. "It was only yesterday that Andrew H. Burke walked, talked, smiled and sighed with us here in Roswell. Only yesterday that he was a part of the life of this little city. There was never a man who was more a part of the social fabric of the community in which he lived than Governor Burke. His was a genial, social nature. He loved his friends, all mankind was his friends and his friends loved him. He loved children, books and flowers and music. He loved company and the company was always brighter and happier for his presence. He radiated warmth and cheer and it was good for the soul to come under the presence of his unfailing optimism. A knight of olden days, a kindly gentleman has gone from among us. Right well he played his part. He laughed with us when we were happy and sighed with us when we were sad.

CHAPTER VIII

A Letter from Andrew H. Burke to The Children's Aid Society

Tell the boys I am proud of them to have had as humble a beginning in life as they, and I believe it has been my salvation. I hope my success in life—if it can be termed—will be an incentive to them to struggle for a respectable recognition among their fellow man. In this country family name cuts but little figure. It is character of the man that wins recognition, hence I would urge them to build carefully and consistently for the future, by being obedient, studious, and manly, thereby inculcating the attributes which tend to make the coming year's efforts successful. Tell them that no one can wish them more happiness than I.

To the boys under your charge, please convey to them my best wishes, and I hope their pathways in life will be those of morality, of honor, of health and industry. With these 4 attributes as guidance and incentive, I can bespeak for them an honorable, happy and successful life. The goal is for them, as well as to the rich man's son.

They must learn "to labor and to wait, for all things cometh to him who waits." Many times the road will be rugged, winding and long, and the sky overcast with ominous clouds. Still it will not do to fall by the wayside and give up. If one does the battle of life will be lost. I attribute my little success in life to a few simple rules, to wit: To be honest, to be truthful, to be industrious in all the byways of life: to be a student, even in a small way, when the opportunity presents itself; to be forgiving and generous to mankind in general; and to follow the Golden Rule-"Do unto others as you would have them do unto you." It is not always sunshine and balm. "Some days will be dark and dreary and into each life some rain must fall," tis then the philosophy of life confronts us, and we take our reckonings, and find whether we are adrift.

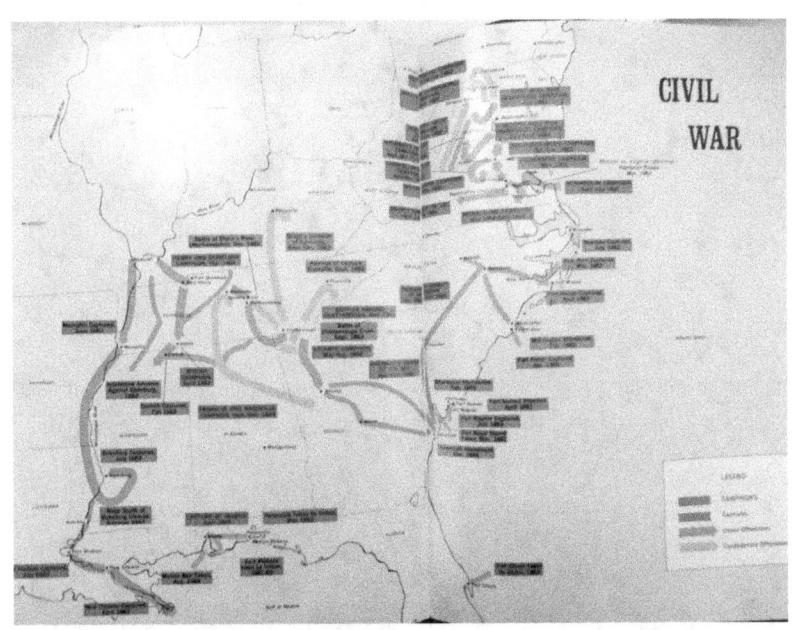

The Civil War, 1861-1865, would cost over 620,000 casualties, making it by far America's deadliest war.

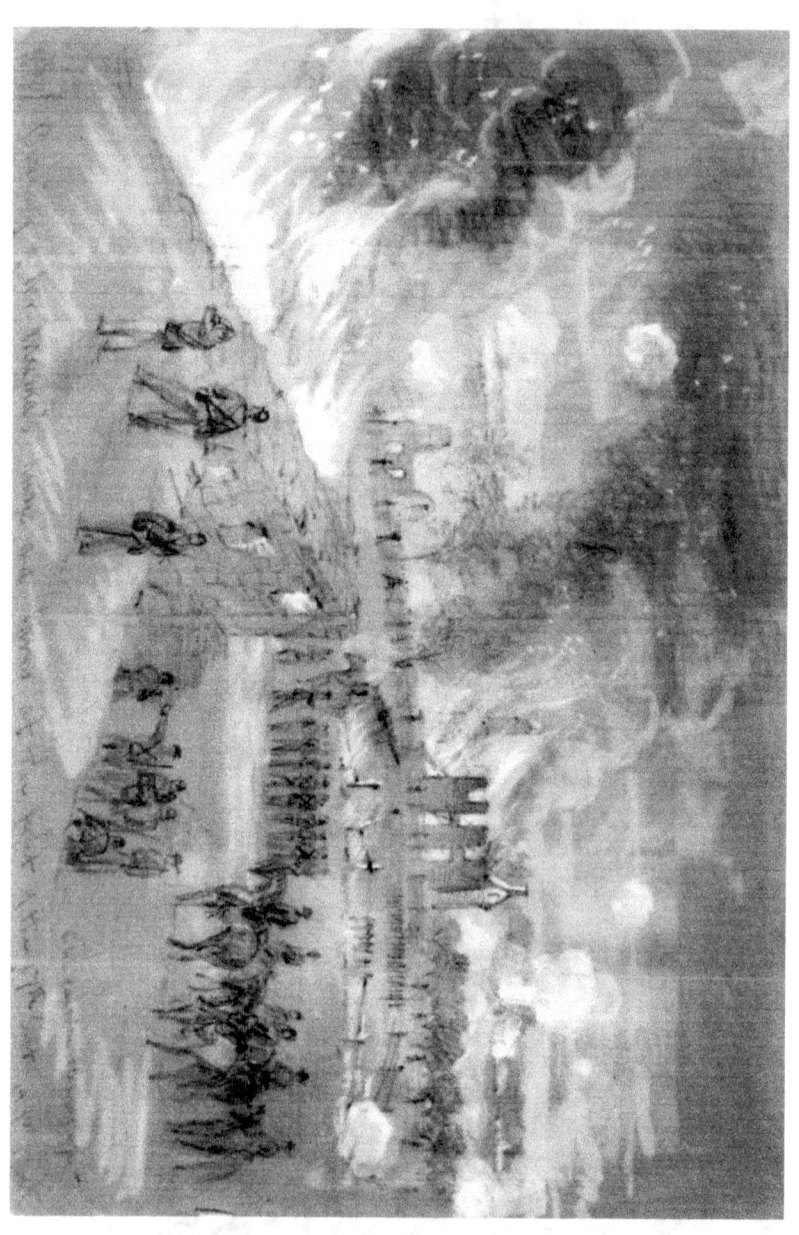

Confederates set the Mumme Farm ablaze.

"WHISTLING DICK"—THE PET OF THE CONFEDERATE GUNNERS

The carnage of the Civil War was terrible.

Caring for the wounded.

Andersonville was the worst confederate prison.

A union victory.

Confederate victory at Fredericksburg.

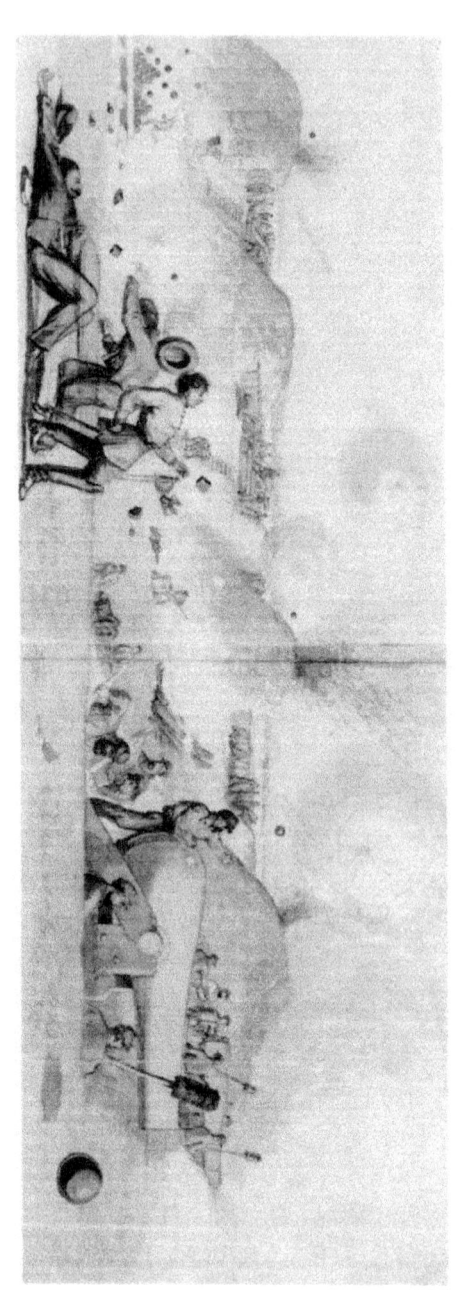

Inside Fort Fisher.

Looking for the wounded.

A Wounded Union Soldier by Winslow Homer.

Freed slaves following union troops.

A freed slave after the Battle of Chancellorsville.

Union retreat at Shiloh.

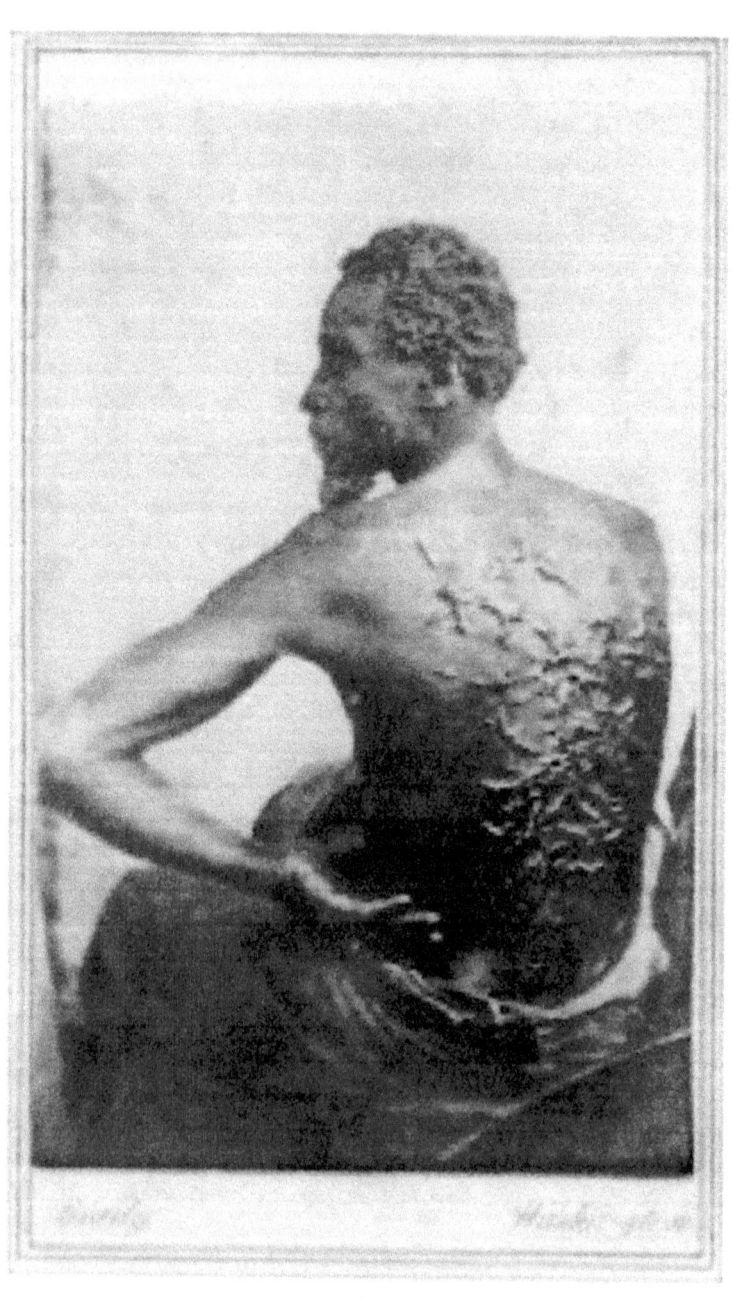

A Louisiana slave showing whip marks.

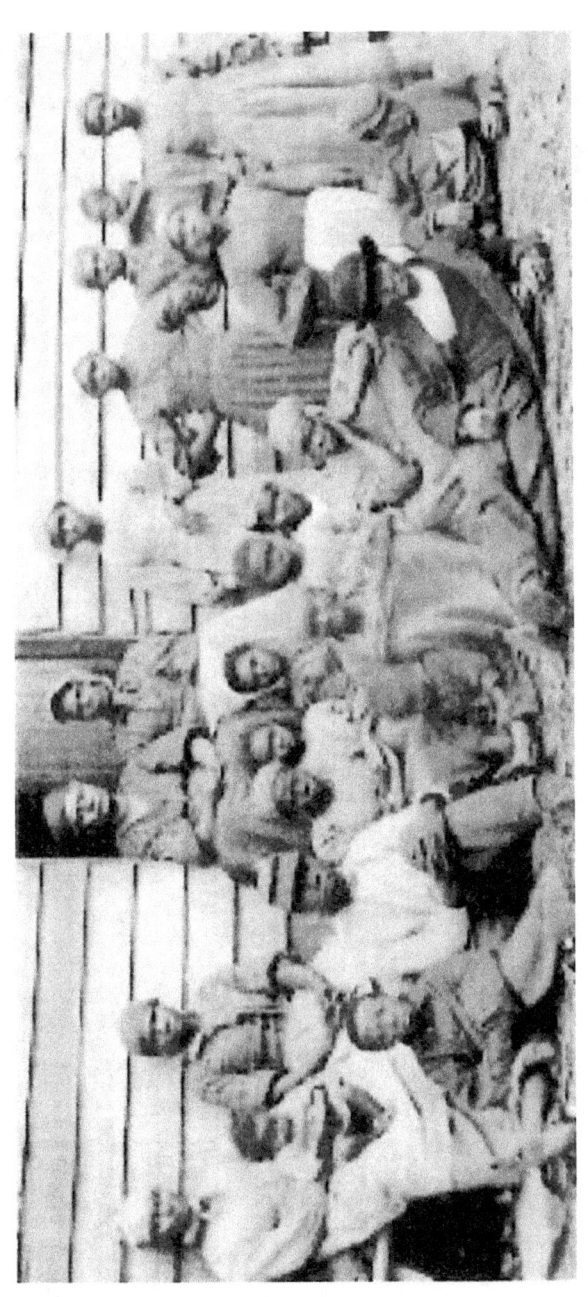

A slave family gathering.

Civil War carnage.

Commander of union forces General Ulysses S. Grant.

Colored union troops.

General William Tecumseh Sherman.

Grant accepts Lee's surrender at Appomattox.

A union soldier.

President Abraham Lincoln.

Celebration over the end of the Civil War.

tered "street arabs" in New York were recorded und 1888 by reformer Jacob Riis. Appalling plight of homeless youths resulted in an exodus on "orphan trains" that survivors recall with mixed emotions.

Please help up to keep the memory of the 273,000 children who rode the Orphan Trains from Grand Central Station in New York City all across America from 1853 to 1929 in search of home and a warm family.

Join our Capital Campaign to Restore the Historic Presidential Landmark Station. It was a time when President Theodore Roosevelt traveled to and from his home at Sagamore Hill in Oyster Bay, New York, to New York City, Washington, D.C., and beyond by train when magnificent steam locomotives plied the rails and their melodious whistles echoed through the countryside.

The rehabilitation of the Historic Landmark Station will prevent further deterioration and restore the building to its circa 1900 appearance. It will fulfill the fundamental mission of the museum to educate and inspire students through the exploration of railroad displays and exhibits and artifacts that school groups will enjoy. It will foster economic growth and connect the waterfront to downtown. The new exhibition gallery will use the latest interactive technology that will inspire a passion for railroading and the past.

Please call John Specce, President of the Oyster Bay Railroad Museum at 516-532-3081 to donate funds, artifacts and time.

OYSTER BAY RAILROAD MUSEUM · STATION showing PARK ENTRANCE

The New Exhibitions Gallery

When completed, the station will feature an exhibitions gallery dedicated to simul[...] [...]ring and entertaining through the accurate interpretation of our collection and exhi[...] [...] way. Whether a child or an adult has a passion for railroading or is attracted to t[...] [...] that made railroading possible, they will find a lasting connection at the Oyster Bay R[...] [...]seum.

Preliminary conceptual renderings of the restored station interior with exhibits (courtesy of Blumlein Associates, Inc.).

A portion of the Gallery will be dedicated to a Visitors Center. Museum personnel will provide information on the many attractions in the Oyster Bay area.

ORPHAN TRAINS